Molly Rides the School Bus

written & illustrated by Julie Brillhart

Albert Whitman & Company

Morton Grove, Illinois

To M. H. and D. G., and with thanks to
Maureen, the bus driver. — J. B.

Library of Congress Cataloging-in-Publication Data
Brillhart, Julie.
Molly rides the school bus / written and illustrated by Julie Brillhart.
p. cm.
Summary: Molly is worried about riding the school bus on her first day
of kindergarten, but a friendly older girl helps her adjust.
ISBN 0-8075-5210-0
[1. School buses — Fiction. 2. First day of school — Fiction.
3. Kindergarten — Fiction. 4. Schools — Fiction.] I. Title.
PZ7.B7666 Mo 2002
[E] — dc21 2001004164

The design is by Scott Piehl.

For more information about Albert Whitman & Company,
please visit our web site at www.albertwhitman.com.

Today was the first day of kindergarten, and Molly was worried. She had never been on the school bus, and she didn't know what to do.

"What if I have to sit with a big kid?" she asked her mom.

"Don't worry, Pumpkin," said her mom. "Big kids are nice, and riding the school bus is fun!"

But Molly wasn't so sure. She didn't really know any big kids. She'd only seen them at the corner store in her neighborhood.

"And besides," continued her mom, "you've got your bear, Willy, with you. You can always sit with him."

"Right," said Molly. She never went anywhere without Willy.

At seven-twenty-five, Molly and her mom waited at the bus stop. A big girl was waiting there, too.

"Hi, I'm Ruby," she said.

Molly didn't answer. She looked away.

"Instead of worrying," said her mom, "why don't you show me how fast those new red sneakers can run."

"No," said Molly. She didn't feel like running.

Just then the big yellow school bus rumbled up. After hugs and kisses for Molly and Willy, Molly waved goodbye to her mom.

"Welcome aboard!" said the bus driver. Molly grabbed the handrail and started up the big steps. She had to lift her knees up high to reach them. "These are the biggest steps I ever took!" she said to Willy.

Inside the bus everyone was talking and laughing. Molly inched her way down the aisle, glancing shyly at all the new faces.

She found an empty seat toward the back of the bus and quickly slid right over to the window. She had just enough time to wave a timid little wave to her mom before the bus roared off . . . VROOMMMM!

Molly missed her mom already. But there was no turning back now. She took off her backpack and reached for Willy. WILLY WASN'T THERE!

She looked frantically all around. "Oh, no!" she cried. "Willy's gone!"

Molly looked up and down the aisle and didn't see Willy anywhere. She looked at the other kids for help, but she was too afraid to say anything.

Molly felt like crying.

Suddenly someone shouted.
Molly looked up, and there was Willy, turning somersaults in the air!

She watched as Willy came down and popped up again and again. Molly reached up to catch Willy, but...

he was tossed from seat to seat and landed "kerplunk" right in a boy's lap.

"Cool!" said the boy. "Nice landing!"

He settled Willy on his knees. "My little sister, Rosie, would LOVE you," he said. "Maybe I'll take you home with me."

"No," said the girl next to him. "The bear should go into the lost-and-found box."

"You're right," said the boy, and he tossed Willy over the seat and into the lost-and-found box.

Lost and Found

"Settle down, everyone!" called the bus driver.
The bus got quiet. Willy rode along next to the driver.

Molly peeked over her seat, wondering what had become of him.

At the next stop, Ruby, who was sitting in the very front seat, got up and lifted Willy out of the box.

"Hey, I know where you belong," she said, and she walked down the aisle to Molly's seat.

Ruby sat down by Molly. It turned out that she was in the fourth grade and knew EVERYTHING about riding the school bus.

"One time," said Ruby, "I was running late and I missed the bus. So my mother drove me to school . . . in her pajamas! All the kids saw her, too. Don't EVER be late!"

Molly laughed.

As the bus bounced along, Ruby admired
all of Molly's new school supplies.

She let Molly listen
to her new CD,

and she shared a piece
of bubble gum that she
found in her pocket.

Molly felt much better now. She held Willy up close and whispered into his ear, "Mom was right, Willy. Big kids ARE nice, and riding the school bus is fun!"

When they arrived at school, Molly followed Ruby out of the bus. "Hey, Ruby," said Molly. "Do you want to see how fast my new red sneakers can run?"

Ruby laughed. "Sure."

And Molly was off in a flash.

RUBY'S TEN TIPS FOR RIDING THE SCHOOL BUS

1.
Get to the bus stop
five minutes early.

2.
Dress properly for
the weather.

3.
When crossing the
street to board or leave
the bus, walk ten feet
in front of the bus.

4.
Hold onto the handrail while
getting on or off.

5.
Stay in your seat
while riding.
If your bus has
seat belts, wear them.

6.

Keep the aisle clear.

7.

Don't throw anything
out the window.

8.

After school, look for
your bus number in the
front window.

9.

In an emergency, use the
emergency door.

10.

Have fun!

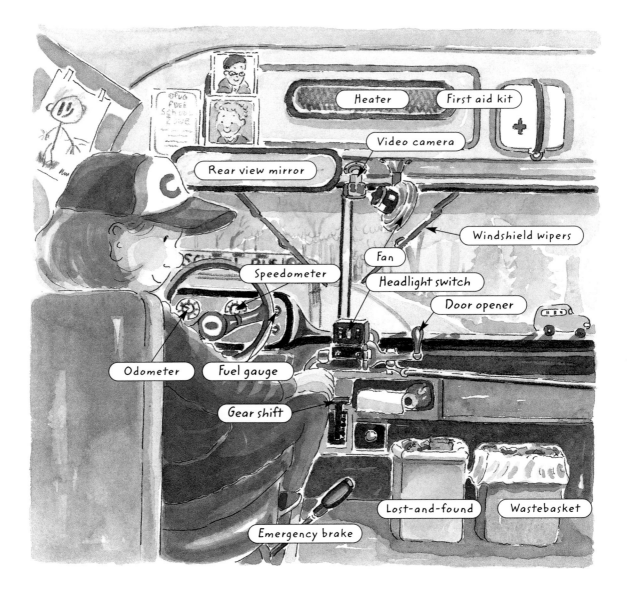